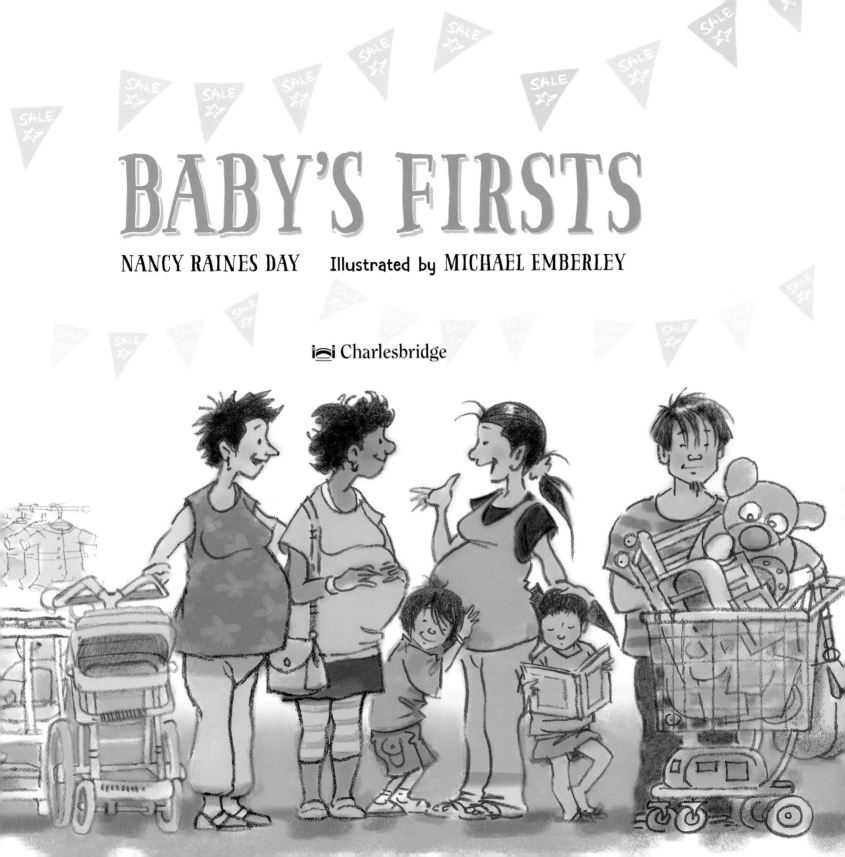

BABY'S FIRSTS

NANCY RAINES DAY   Illustrated by MICHAEL EMBERLEY

ini Charlesbridge

First cry.

First meal.

First burp.

Warm feel.

First poop,
           first pee.

                        First change,

pew-ee!

All snug

on lap.

First song,

then nap.

First grab,

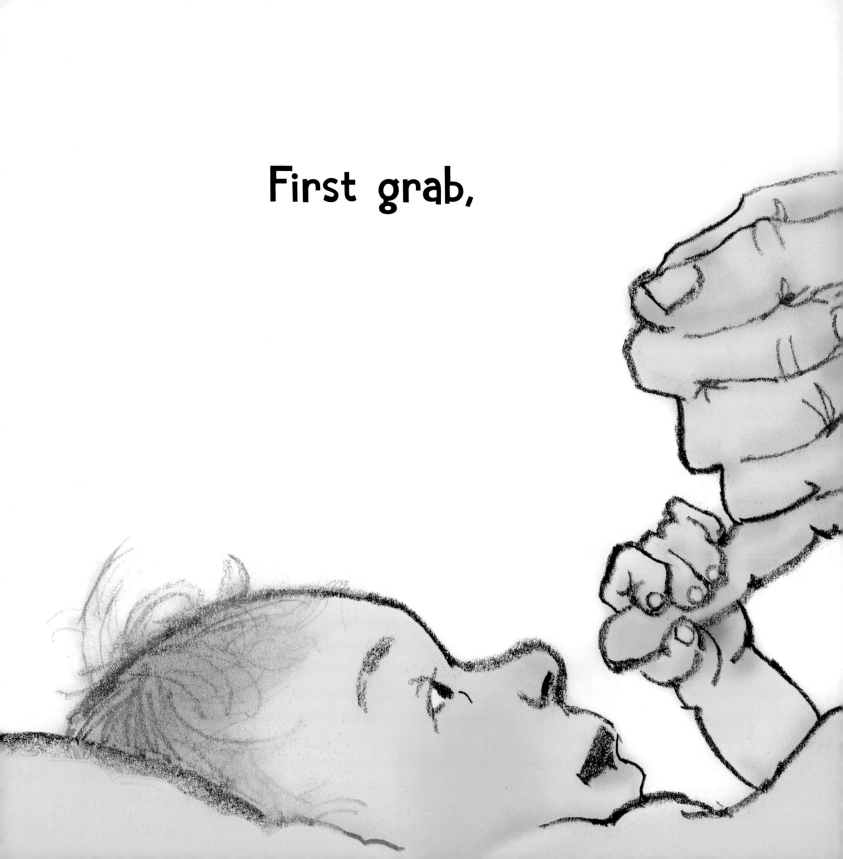

first smile.

First laugh.

What style!

First teeth.
First bite.

Need bath
tonight.

First roll,

then creep.

First crawl,

then sleep.

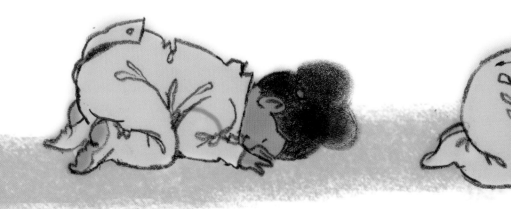

First game.

First ride.

First swing.

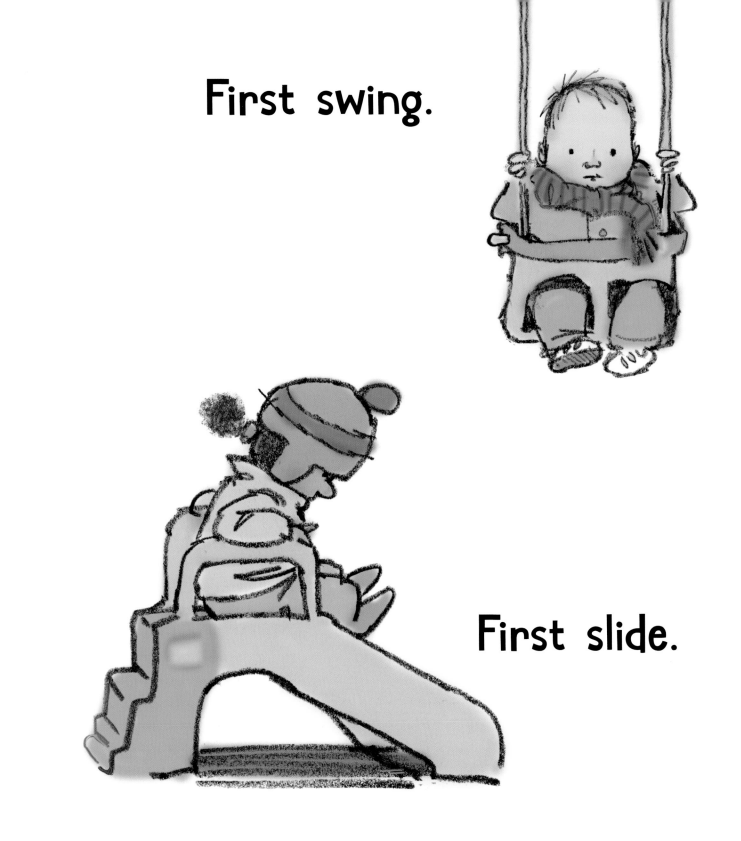

First slide.

First step,

then walk.

First word,

then talk.

What fun,
first year.

First birthday
is here!

To Phyllis, who's enjoying her grandbaby's firsts—N. R. D.

For Debbie: Ar dheis Dé go raibh a hanam—M. E.

Published by Charlesbridge, 85 Main Street, Watertown, MA 02472
(617) 926-0329 · www.charlesbridge.com

Library of Congress Cataloging-in-Publication Data
Names: Day, Nancy Raines, author. | Emberley, Michael, illustrator.
Title: Baby's firsts / Nancy Raines Day ; illustrated by Michael Emberley.
Description: Watertown, MA: Charlesbridge, [2018] | Summary: Told in rhyming text,
the story traces the development of three babies from birth to their first birthday.
Identifiers: LCCN 2016053953 (print) | LCCN 2017010215 (ebook) | ISBN 9781580897747
(reinforced for library use) | ISBN 9781632896377 (ebook) | ISBN 9781632896384 (ebook pdf)
Subjects: LCSH: Infants—Development—Juvenile fiction. | Stories in rhyme.|
CYAC: Stories in rhyme. | Babies—Fiction. | LCGFT: Stories in rhyme.
Classification: LCC PZ8.3.D3334 Bab 2018 (print) | LCC PZ8.3.D3334 (ebook) |
DDC [E]—dc23
LC record available at https://lccn.loc.gov/2016053953

Printed in China
(hc) 10 9 8 7 6 5 4 3 2 1
Illustrations done in pencil on paper, using several sketchbooks, digital color, and lots of coffee
Type set in Digby, designed by Amy Dietrich for Atlantic Fonts
Color separations by Colourscan Print Co Pte Ltd, Singapore
Printed by 1010 Printing International Limited in Huizhou, Guangdong, China
Production supervision by Brian G. Walker
Designed by Susan Mallory Sherman